Written and Illustrated

by Marie Le Tourneau

with Danielle Reed Baty

Tanglewood Press —— Terre Haute, IN

in loving memory of
my grandmother
Marie Lucy Girardi
and for my grandpa,
Charlie,
"and how!"
—mL

To Julie,
with love,
Maman et Papa

—DR

Published by Tanglewood Press, Inc., June 2006.

Designed by Allison Higa Design
Editorial assistance provided by Lisa Rojany Buccieri

The publisher wishes to thank Jean-Philippe Baty for his assistance with this book.

Tanglewood Press, Inc. P. O. Box 3009, Terre Haute, IN 47803 www.tanglewoodbooks.com

Printed in China
10 9 8 7 6 5 4 3 2 1

ISBN-10 0-9749303-6-9
ISBN-13 978-0-97493036-7

Library of Congress Cataloging-in-Publication Data

Le Tourneau, Marie.
  The mice of Bistrot des Sept Frères / written and illustrated by Marie
Le Tourneau with Danielle Reed Baty.
    p. cm.
  Summary: Petite Michelle comes to the rescue when the chef at a famous Parisian restaurant for mice runs out of the secret ingredient in his prize-winning cheese soup. Story is interspersed with French words.
    ISBN-13: 978-0-9749303-6-7 (alk. paper)
    ISBN-10: 0-9749303-6-9 (alk. paper)
  [1. Mice--Fiction. 2. Restaurants-- Fiction. 3. Soups--Fiction. 4. Paris (France)-- Fiction. 5. France-- Fiction.]   I. Baty, Danielle Reed. II. Title.
PZ7.L454Mi 2006
[E]--dc22
                              2006006341

French Pronunciations

Au fromage (oh FROmahj)

Au revoir (Oh ruhVWAR)

Le bistro(t) (luh beeSTRO)

Le Bistrot des Sept Frères
(luh beeSTRO day set frair)

Bonjour (baw-joor)

Le bouillon (luh bweeYAW)

Cafés express (cafAY exPRESS)

Cher (shair)

La crème (la krem)

Est (ay)

Excellent(e) (ekselAHNT)

Félicitations! (fayleeseetassYAW)

Des fleurs (day flure)

Les frères (lay frair)

Le Maître D'hôtel (luh MAYtra d'ohTELL)

Les oeufs durs (lays euh dure)

Les oignons (lays onYO)

Le pâtissier (luh pateesYAY)

Petit, petite (puhTEE, puhTEET)

Le poivre (luh PWAVruh)

La sauce piquante aux poivrons
(la sose peeKAWNT oh pwavRAW)

Sept (set)

Les serveurs (lay sairVEUR)

Les serviettes de table
(lay sairveeYETTE duh TAHbluh)

La soeur (la sur)

Le sommelier (luh somelYAY)

La soupe (la soup)

Le sous-chef (luh SUE chef)

Le thym (luh TEH)

Très bien! (tray byeh)

Voilà (vwaLA)

In Paris' Latin Quarter, Chef Marcel owns a fancy
bistro called *Le Bistrot des Sept Frères,* or The Bistro
of the Seven Brothers.
   Le Bistrot des Sept Frères has the very best in mouse cuisine.
Anyone who is anyone eats there. It is the hippest place in Paris!

Chef Marcel is known throughout France for his wonderfully delicious *soupe au fromage*, cheese soup.

The cheese soup is made with a very special, secret ingredient known only to Chef Marcel. Every year, the bistro wins the big award for the best cheese soup in all of France. The bistro is always busy, but Chef Marcel has plenty of help in the kitchen from his seven sons.

Les Trois Sous-Chefs
(The Three Assistant Chefs)

This is Jean-Pierre. He loves boating.

The twins, Jean-Paul and Jean-Henri, adore skiing in alpine races.

Jean-Philippe plays a mean bass in a blues band.

Jean-Michel is truly fond of relaxing by the sea.

Les Deux Serveurs
(The Two Waiters)

Jean-Marc writes sensitive poetry.

Jean-Alexandre kicks a cool soccer ball.

And last but not least, there is Chef Marcel's youngest child, his only daughter, Petite Michelle, who loves the ballet. She helps out here and there.

Each morning, Chef Marcel calls his sons together and says, "Tell me the recipe for our wonderful cheese soup."

And the sons recite: "Butter, cheese, stock, cream, onion, pepper, thyme, and the secret ingredient."

And Chef Marcel says, *"Très bien!"*, which means: very good.

One day, a telegram arrives at the bistro.

MOUSE UNION
TELEGRAM

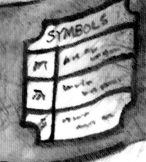

Cher Chef Marcel,

It is that time of year again!

French Culinary Judge Alfred Le Whisk

will arrive at your bistro

to taste your famous cheese soup

on the 2nd of June,

at one o'clock sharp.

Best Regards as ever,

The Committee for the Best

cheese Soup in All of France.

"Oh no!" cries Chef Marcel. "That is one hour from now, and I am out of the secret ingredient!" His cry makes Jean-Marc and Jean-Alexandre run to the kitchen, where they bump into Jean-Michel,
which makes Jean-Michel drop a bottle of cider,
which makes Jean-Paul and Jean-Henri upset a bowl of cream,
which makes Jean-Philippe drop the bread,
which makes Jean-Pierre toss the onions into the air!

Calmly, Petite Michelle puts hard-boiled eggs — *les oeufs durs* — in a basket on the corner of the bar.

"I have to go to the market to get the secret ingredient. While I am gone, everyone must help to make the soup," instructs Chef Marcel.

Jean-Pierre melts the cheese
—*le fromage.*

Jean-Paul and Jean-Henri add
the cream—*la crème.*

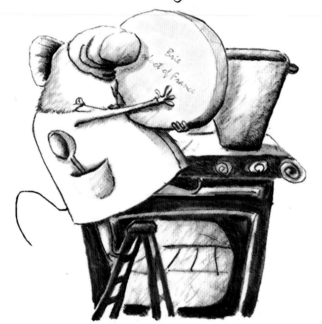

Jean-Alexandre makes
the stock—*le bouillon.*

Jean-Marc cuts fresh thyme—*le thym.*

Jean-Philippe chops
the onions—*les oignons.*

Jean-Michel adds the pepper—*le poivre.*

And Petite Michelle folds the napkins — *les serviettes de table* — just so.

At five minutes to one, Chef Marcel has not yet returned.
"What will we do?" cries Jean-Pierre.
His cry makes Jean-Marc and Jean-Alexandre run
into the kitchen, where they bump into Jean-Paul,
which makes Jean-Paul toss peas and carrots into the air,
which makes Jean-Henri upset a bowl of broccoli,
which makes Jean-Philippe slip and drop a cake,
which makes Jean-Michel lose his grip on a tray
of *cafés express*!

Without a word, Petite Michelle walks over to the stove—*la cuisinière.*

She adds a dash of salt . . . a bit of rosemary . . .

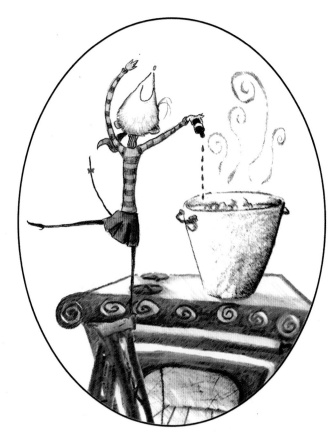

and six drops of hot pepper sauce—*sauce piquante aux poivrons.*

Voilà! The soup is ready!

At the stroke of one, Alfred Le Whisk arrives at the bistro.
"Bonjour, monsieur," says Petite Michelle.

Jean-Pierre pours the soup into a bowl.
Jean-Paul carries the pot.
Jean-Henri adds the garnish.
Jean-Philippe puts the bread in a basket.
Jean-Marc and Jean-Alexandre lay out the napkins.
Jean-Michel pours the cider.

Casually, over in the corner, Petite Michelle arranges some flowers—*des fleurs*—in a vase.

Alfred Le Whisk's stomach growls. He lifts a spoonful of soup to his mouth. Everyone holds their breath. Just then, Chef Marcel arrives, completely out of breath. It is too late. Monsieur Le Whisk has swallowed.

"Judge Le Whisk! *S'il vous plaît*, please, let me explain—"

But the judge interrupts him.

"Chef Marcel, before I decide whose soup is the best of the best, I must know. What do you put in your soup?"

Chef Marcel looks at his sons. His sons look back at him. Petite Michelle says nothing. Judge Le Whisk pats his mouth with his napkin.

"Er . . ." says Chef Marcel. "Why don't we tell the judge what we put in our wonderful cheese soup?"

The Jeans begin to recite the ingredients.
"Butter, cheese, stock, cream, onion,
pepper, thyme, and . . ."

"And?" questioned the judge.
There was nothing but silence.

Suddenly a soft voice spoke out.

"A dash of salt . . .

a bit of rosemary . . .

and six drops of hot pepper sauce!"

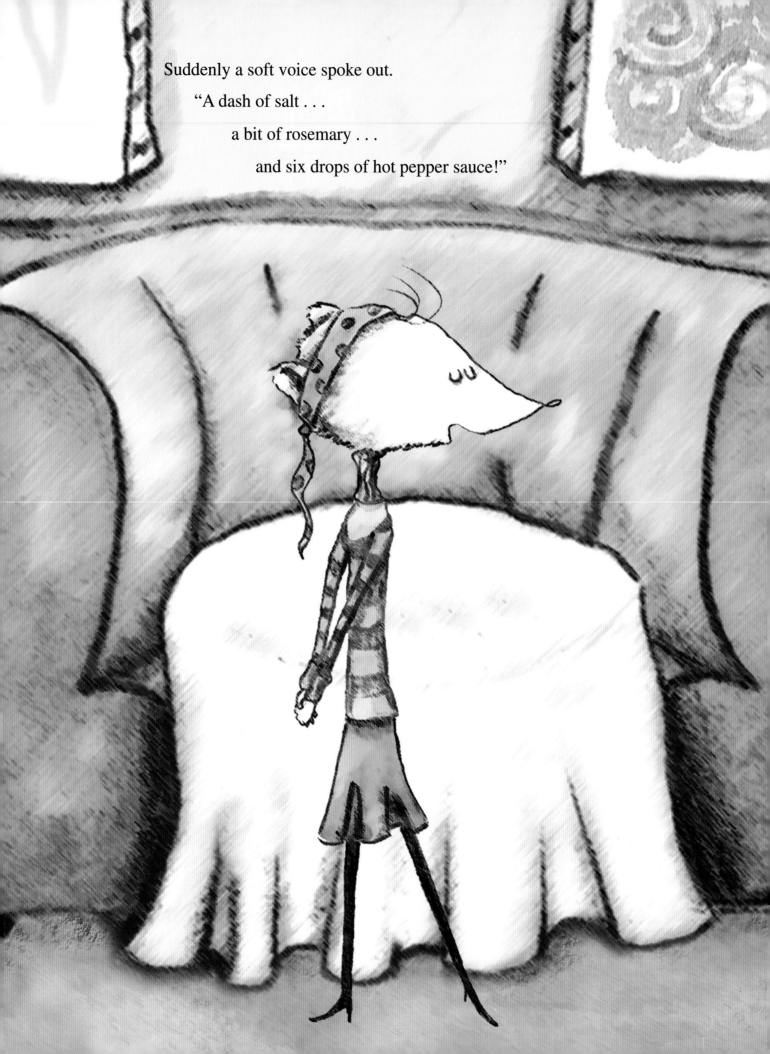

Judge Le Whisk frowns. He wipes his mouth with his napkin.
Every beady little eye in the room is on him—
and he knows it.

"Chef Marcel, your soup
was good before, but . . ."

"But what?" asks
Chef Marcel.

"But this time, your new cheese soup is not only the
best in France, but the best in all the world! *Félicitations*!"

Chef Marcel jumps for joy.

Then he bows.

"*Merci*, Judge Le Whisk!"

His sons dance around the bistro.
"Three cheers for Petite Michelle! Hurrah! Hurrah! Hurrah!"
Petite Michelle saves the day . . . and the soup!

As for Judge Le Whisk . . .

he asks for a second helping!
"*Merci*!" he says. "*La soupe est excellente!*"

(The Bistro of the Seven Brothers and One Sister)

P.S.: Do you agree with the mice in Paris that the soup is yummy? Make it yourself and find out! The recipe is at www.tanglewoodbooks.com.